Rochamb

THE SWORD IN THE GROTTO

~2~
ARAMINTA SPOOKIE
THE SWORD IN THE GROTTO

as told to
ANGIE SAGE

illustrated by
JIMMY PICKERING

KATHERINE TEGEN BOOKS
An Imprint of HarperCollins*Publishers*

Araminta Spookie 2: The Sword in the Grotto

Copyright © 2006 by Angie Sage

Illustrations copyright © 2006 by Jimmy Pickering

Library of Congress Cataloging-in-Publication Data

Sage, Angie.

The sword in the grotto / Angie Sage ; illustrated by Jimmy Pickering.— 1st ed.

p.   cm.

"Araminta Spookie 2."

Sequel to: My haunted house.

Summary: With the help of the ghost Edmund, Araminta and Wanda survive a trip through a secret tunnel to bring back a present for Sir Horace's birthday.

ISBN-10: 0-06-077484-3 (trade bdg.)

ISBN-13: 978-0-06-077484-4 (trade bdg.)

ISBN-10: 0-06-077485-1 (lib. bdg.)

ISBN-13: 978-0-06-077485-1 (lib. bdg.)

[1. Ghosts—Fiction. 2. Adventure and adventures—Fiction.] I. Pickering, Jimmy, ill. II. Title.

PZ7.S13035Swo 2006   2005023816

[Fic]—dc22   CIP

                                                                              AC

Typography by Amy Ryan

1 2 3 4 5 6 7 8 9 10

❖

First Edition

For
Araminta Clibborn,
with love

CONTENTS

THE SWORD IN THE GROTTO

~1~

SHIRLEY

Spookie House, which is where I live with my aunt Tabitha and my uncle Drac, has recently gotten pretty crowded. First of all I found two ghosts living here, and then the Wizzards turned up and decided to live here too. So now that makes eight of us, as there are three Wizzards—Wanda and her mom and dad, Brenda and Barry.

Our two ghosts are Sir Horace and

Edmund. Most people think that Sir Horace is just a boring old suit of armor—which is what I thought for ages—but he is our biggest ghost. Then there is his faithful page, Edmund, who is shy and acts like he's a bit of a wimp. Wanda really likes him, but she *would*, as she can be a bit of a wimp too, as you will see.

Sometimes I think Sir Horace likes Wanda better than me. Not that I am jealous or anything, even though Sir Horace was *my* ghost first. But after the Wizzards came to live here, they repaired Sir Horace so that he looked almost like new, and Wanda got rid of all Sir Horace's rust with her bike oil, which he was really pleased about. After that, Sir Horace walked around a lot more than he used to. He didn't creak anymore either, which was a bit weird, as sometimes you might be just hanging around planning an ambush for Aunt Tabby or something, and suddenly there would be Sir Horace, standing right behind you.

But last month Sir Horace stopped walking around and started getting sulky. He took to lurking behind some revolting old curtains on the landing, and one night he really frightened Uncle Drac when he let out a horrible groan just as Uncle Drac was coming out of his turret.

Another time Sir Horace deliberately took his head off and left it on the stairs. Aunt Tabby tripped over it and blamed *me*. When I gave him his head back, he was not polite at all. He told me that he was trying to forget something and he didn't want his head just then, thank you very much. But I made him put it back on. After that he disappeared. We looked everywhere, but we couldn't find him, so Wanda and I went down to his secret room to see if he was there.

To get to Sir Horace's room, you have to go through a secret passage and then down in a funny old elevator, called a dumbwaiter, which you have to work yourself by pulling on a rope. Wanda and I are not allowed to go there, as Aunt Tabby says the elevator is dangerous, and she does not like us hanging around in secret passages. But the real reason is that Aunt Tabby does not like people being anywhere where she cannot see what they are doing, as she is extremely nosy.

But even though Aunt Tabby is so nosy, she does not know everything. For example, she does not know that I have the key to the door to the secret passage. So yesterday, when Wanda and I were sure that Aunt Tabby was safely out of the way, we opened the secret door, which is in the paneling under the attic stairs. We walked along the secret passage. I had to go first because of the spiders—which Wanda does not like—then we went down in the creaky elevator—which Wanda does not like—and went into Sir Horace's room.

The room was very small and dark—Wanda did not like that, either. But I don't know what else she expected, as there are no windows in it because it is a *secret* room in the middle of the house. I shone my flashlight into all the corners to see if Sir Horace was sulking there while Wanda looked scared.

"He's not here," said Wanda. "I hope he hasn't run away."

"Why would he do that?" I asked.

"He likes it at our house. Can I have the cheese and onion chips?"

Wanda was carrying our Secret Passage Kit, and she gave me my bag of cheese and onion chips. Then she lit the two candles above the fireplace. They cast strange shadows on the walls, and I made a big monster shadow loom over her.

Wanda, who is even more nosy than my aunt Tabby, started looking through all the old books that were piled up. They were very boring, and I didn't know why she was bothering, but Wanda likes boring old stuff— which is why she likes Sir Horace, I suppose. Anyway, suddenly Wanda snorted like a pig inhaling its food and started rolling around the floor. I didn't take any notice, as I know that this is Wanda's way of laughing. So I let her do her pig impression for a bit, and then I asked her what was so funny.

"Oink oink oink," snorted Wanda, "oh, *oink*!"

"Oh, come on, Wanda. Tell me."

Wanda shoved a funny old book into my hands. "Shirley," she snorted. "Oink oink. *Shirley*!"

Inside the book was an old piece of paper with a picture someone had drawn of a cute baby lying on a rug. Underneath the picture was some spidery writing. It was not very easy to read.

"Go on . . . *oink*," snorted Wanda. "Read it."

"Er . . . 'Horace Cuthbert Shirley George, age foure monthe,'" I read out. "Their spelling was terrible in the old days, wasn't it?"

"Not as bad as yours," oinked Wanda. "See? He's called *Shirley*."

"Well, maybe his mom wanted a girl or

something. Anyway, I think he looks sweet. But that can't be Sir Horace. He was never a baby."

Wanda managed to sit up. "Everyone was a baby once," she said. "Even my dad was a baby once, although that was ages ago. Probably about the same time as when Sir Horace was a baby."

"Your dad may be old, but I don't think he's nearly five hundred years old," I said, staring at the date in the book.

"He might be," Wanda said. "I wouldn't be surprised. What are you doing?"

"Counting," I told her. Math is not one of my best subjects, and I was counting up on my fingers to make sure I had it right. One hundred, two hundred, three hundred, four hundred . . . Hey it *was* right—the day after tomorrow it will be five hundred years exactly since Sir Horace was born!

"The day after tomorrow is Sir Horace's birthday," I said. "His *five-hundredth* birthday."

Wanda whistled. "That's a *big* birthday."

"The biggest birthday ever," I said. "I mean, who else do you know who has had a five-hundredth birthday?"

Wanda thought for a while and then she said, "I don't think I know anyone. That is *so* old. Hey—that's why he's sulking. My dad did that last year. He had what Mom called a big birthday, and he got really funny the week before. He turned all his frogs blue and he wouldn't talk to anyone. But he cheered up at his surprise birthday party. He was fine after that."

I finished eating my cheese and onion chips, and then suddenly I had a Plan. "Problem solved," I said. "We'll give Sir Horace a surprise five-hundredth birthday party, and then he'll be fine too."

Wanda smiled. I could see she was impressed with my brilliant Plan. And then she stopped smiling and said, "But we don't know where he is. You have to know where someone is if you want to give him a surprise party. Otherwise you end up having a party and he's not there to be surprised. And then it's not a surprise party; it's just a——"

"All right, *all right*," I said. "I get the point."

Trust Wanda to make things difficult.

~2~

THUD

"Sir Horace will soon come out of wherever he's hiding when he hears he's having a surprise party," I told Wanda. We were on our way down to the third-kitchen-on-the-left-just-past-the-boiler-room to check out the party food situation.

"It won't be a surprise if he hears about it," said Wanda. She is what my Uncle Drac calls "pedantic." I am not sure what that means,

but it sounds about right for Wanda, if you ask me. Plus you can add picky to that.

"Anyway, we don't *have* to have a surprise party for him," Wanda said. "Perhaps he would like to drive a race car or something. My mom did that when she turned forty. And Sir Horace already has his own crash helmet."

I wasn't so sure about that. Something told me that Sir Horace and racing cars would not go together well.

"Or we could just get him a really good present," said Wanda. "But it's no good buying him a pair of socks because he's got no feet. Or aftershave because he doesn't shave. Or handkerchiefs because he's got no nose, or boxer shorts because he's got no—"

"Yeah, yeah, I know. There's no need to go on and *on*, Wanda," I told her. Sometimes

Wanda does not know when to stop.

The party food was no problem. Brenda had a whole cupboard stuffed full of chips and candy. In fact, it was so full that when Wanda opened the door, a torrent of bags of gummi bears fell on our heads. One of them burst, so we had to eat all the bears, as Aunt Tabby always says, "If *you* make a mess, Araminta, *you* clean it up."

We had very nearly cleaned up all the bears when a massive *THUD* echoed through the walls of the kitchen. It rocked the cupboard, and another shower of gummi bears leaped out and hit Wanda on the head.

"Ouch! Wharrer*at*?" she said.

"I don't know, do I?" I told her. Wanda still thinks I know what's going on in this house, but I don't.

Wanda gulped down the last of the bears. "It sounded like someone heaved a huge sack of potatoes out of a window right at the top of the house," she said.

"Don't be ridiculous," I told her. "Who would want to throw a huge sack of potatoes out of the— Uncle Drac!" Suddenly I just *knew* what had happened. I ran out the door and crashed straight into Aunt Tabby.

"It's Drac!" yelled Aunt Tabby. "Come on, Araminta—quick!" Aunt Tabby picked herself up from the floor and zoomed off around the corner and along the long corridor that winds through the basement. I couldn't see her very well, as all the lights in the corridor burned out years ago and she always wears black, but that didn't matter. I knew exactly where she was headed—to the bat turret poo hatch.

Wanda was close behind me. "Why," she puffed, "would Uncle Drac want to throw a sack of potatoes out of a window? And what's the fuss, anyway? We can always pick them up. Potatoes don't break or anything. It's not like he threw a sack of eggs out of the—"

"Oh, be quiet, Wanda," I told her.

Like I said before, Wanda is picky and does not know when to stop. She doesn't think, either, because if Wanda had stopped to think for one moment, she would have realized that the *THUD* we heard was Uncle Drac in his sleeping bag falling four floors down from the top of the bat turret. Which was not a good thing, particularly for Uncle Drac.

Aunt Tabby skidded to a halt at the far end of the corridor. In front of her, at the base of Uncle Drac's bat turret, was the bat poo hatch. It was like a huge and very heavy cat flap. Aunt Tabby heaved it open and grabbed Uncle Drac's shovel, which was leaning up beside it. Then she started digging.

Aunt Tabby was like a dog digging for its bone. Bat poo flew everywhere as she frantically heaved great shovel loads out of the hatch. I got out of the way quickly, but Wanda, who had not seen the hatch before, was not as fast.

"Eeow!" she yelled as a large shovelful of bat poo splattered over her. "That's disgusting!"

"Shh, Wanda," said Aunt Tabby, "I thought I heard Drac. Araminta, can you hear something?"

I listened as more shovelfuls of bat poo flew through the air.

"Errrgh . . ." A faint groaning came from inside the tube.

"Drac, Drac, are you all right?" yelled Aunt Tabby. "Hold on, Drac, we're coming to get you."

"Errrgh . . . arrgh . . ."

"What's he doing in there?" asked Wanda.

"I thought he was upstairs with the potatoes."

"What potatoes?" asked Aunt Tabby suspiciously.

"Don't take any notice of Wanda," I told Aunt Tabby. "Just keep digging."

"Why?" asked Wanda, who is very nosy. "Why doesn't anyone tell me what's going on?"

"Done!" said Aunt Tabby. She had dug a tunnel up through the huge pile of bat poo. She took out her flashlight and shone it up through the tunnel. I could see the rafters right at the top of the turret, where Uncle Drac's sleeping bag usually hangs. It wasn't there.

"Hold the shovel, Araminta," said Aunt Tabby. "I'm going in." So I held the shovel and watched Aunt Tabby scramble through the poo hatch and disappear.

"Errgh," said Wanda, holding her nose. "How can she stand going in there?"

"Because Uncle Drac has just fallen four floors down from the top of the bat turret and she is going to save him, that's why."

Wanda looked surprised. "But I thought you said—"

"And I'm going in to

help her," I said, deciding that crawling through a few tons of bat poo was better than trying to explain anything to Wanda.

Actually, it was a lot worse than explaining anything to Wanda. It smelled revolting, and some of it was horribly soft and squidgy. But I climbed in, and soon I was standing on the floor of the turret. Well, not exactly on the *floor*—on the pile of bat poo that covers the floor. And lying there on the pile of poo was a large, flowery sleeping bag.

"Errrgh . . ." groaned the sleeping bag.

Aunt Tabby was kneeling beside it, and I could see Uncle Drac's white face peering out. He didn't look too good.

"It's all right, Drac," said Aunt Tabby, but she didn't look like it was all right at all.

"No . . . it's not," moaned Uncle Drac.

"Something *terrible* has happened."

"Oh, Drac, dear. Tell me, what—what has happened? What have you done?" Aunt Tabby gasped.

Uncle Drac slowly lifted his head, and Aunt Tabby and I leaned close to hear what he was going to say. We both thought it might be Uncle Drac's *last words*.

"I—I've squashed Big Bat," he groaned.

~3~
THE BROOM
CLOSET

The next morning Aunt Tabby yelled up to our Saturday bedroom, "Uncle Drac's back from the hospital. Two broken legs, nothing to worry about."

I jumped out of bed and looked through the small trapdoor. Aunt Tabby was standing at the bottom of the rope ladder in the corridor below.

"Two broken legs?" I said. "But that's awful, Aunt Tabby."

"Better than having three, dear," she said briskly. "Drac's resting in the broom closet. I want both of you to be very quiet this morning and leave him in peace."

Wanda sat up in bed with her hair sticking up like it always does. "Why is he in the broom closet?" she asked. "Shouldn't he be in bed?"

"Uncle Drac doesn't have a bed, silly," I told her. "He sleeps in his sleeping bag in the bat turret."

"Why?" asked Wanda, rubbing her eyes.

"I don't know. Because he likes being with his bats, I suppose. Come on, let's go and see him."

"But Aunt Tabby said—"

"Duh," I told her. "You don't want to take any notice of what Aunt Tabby says. Come on, Wanda. Get up." And I pulled her duvet off.

The broom closet is downstairs by the back door. Barry's frogs were waiting for him outside, and we could hear Barry's voice coming from the closet. He was arguing with Uncle Drac.

"I don't know why you're making such a fuss, Drac," he was saying grumpily. "I told you, I'm going in a minute."

"You promised me you'd deliver it last night," Uncle Drac complained.

"No I didn't," said Barry. "I promised I'd deliver it. I didn't say I'd take the wretched stuff there at midnight. That's ridiculous, Drac."

"It is *not* ridiculous," Uncle Drac growled. "I always deliver it at night. I've been doing it for years. That's when Old Morris expects it, and that's when the mushrooms like it."

"How can you possibly know what mushrooms like?" Barry asked.

"I understand mushrooms," said Uncle Drac. "Me and mushrooms have a lot in common. We both like dark and peace and quiet. Now go away, close the door, and leave me alone."

Barry stomped out of the broom closet and nearly trod on one of his frogs. "I wouldn't go in there," he said to us. "He's in a really bad mood. Would anyone like to take a trip to the mushroom farm? I could use some help." He scooped up his frogs and put them in his pocket.

"I'll come, Dad," said Wanda, and she ran off without even bothering to see how Uncle Drac was.

I pushed open the door to the broom closet and peered in. It was really dark and gloomy in there. Aunt Tabby had put a blanket over the tiny window to keep the light out, as Uncle Drac doesn't like daylight very much. I slipped into the closet and closed the door behind me. All I could see were Uncle Drac's two white plaster casts propped up on a footstool, but Uncle Drac, who can see really well in the dark said, "Hello, Minty. You can put the light on if you like. I may as well get on with my knitting."

"*Knitting*, Uncle Drac?" I was a bit shocked. I didn't know Uncle Drac liked knitting.

"Knitting stops people from moaning— according to Tabby," Uncle Drac said gloomily. He waved a pair of knitting needles and a ball of green yarn at me. "I'd watch it if I were you, Minty. One moan, and she'll have you knitting a scarf too."

I looked at the green muddle of wool on Uncle Drac's knitting needles. "Is that a *scarf*, Uncle Drac?" I asked.

"Of course it's a scarf. Can't you tell?" And then he said, "Minty, would you do me a favor?"

"Of course, Uncle Drac."

"Would you go into the bat turret and see if Big Bat is . . . squashed?"

"Squashed, Uncle Drac?"

"Er, yes. I fell on him last night. And I couldn't see him anywhere when Tabby and Barry got me out."

"Well then, I expect he *is* pretty squashed," I said. "Squished, even. You are quite heavy, Uncle Drac. And *really* heavy compared to a bat."

Uncle Drac groaned.

"Are your legs hurting?" I asked him.

"Big Bat, Minty, Big Bat. Go and find him, will you?"

I didn't reply right away, as I had just seen something rather interesting. A pair of pointy metal feet were sticking out from underneath a pile of coats—I had found out where Sir Horace was hiding! I decided not to say anything to Sir Horace, as I didn't want him to disappear again. I figured if he thought that no one knew where he was, he would stay put.

I left Uncle Drac to his knitting and went to find Big Bat. I didn't want to go and find Big Bat, as I am not that keen on squashed bats myself, and Big Bat would be an awful lot of squashed bat. But I knew that, knitting or not, Uncle Drac would keep asking me about it until I did.

When I got down to the bat poo hatch, I found four sacks of bat poo leaning up against the wall—Barry and Wanda were busy getting Uncle Drac's delivery ready. Uncle Drac runs Drac's Bats. He delivers sacks of bat poo fertilizer to farms, but the bat poo business had not being doing too well lately and Uncle Drac only had one customer left, the Morris Mushroom Farm down by the beach.

I took a deep breath and crawled into the bat poo tunnel. When I got to the top, it was hard to see much. There were bats flying around everywhere, and bat poo was falling like rain.

Barry and Wanda were just filling the last sack. Wanda held the sack open with one hand while holding up a big umbrella in her other hand to keep the showers of poo off her.

"Do you want some help?" I asked.

"Oh, thanks a lot," said Wanda snappily,

"but Dad and I have finished now."

Barry put the last shovelful of poo into the sack, then he and Wanda dragged it down to join the other four in the corridor. I had a quick look for Big Bat, but I couldn't see a thing. Everything was covered with a new layer of poo, and it had all been trampled by Wanda and Barry. Big Bat, I decided, was probably history. But I didn't want to go and tell Uncle Drac that. Not yet, anyway.

"Right," said Barry as I crawled out of the bat poo door, "let's get these sacks into the van."

Barry had driven Uncle Drac's van around to the back door. Wanda and Barry heaved the sacks in, and I told them where to put them. Then Barry and Wanda got in the van. Wanda slammed the door, and Barry started up the engine.

"Hey, what about me?" I banged on Wanda's window.

Wanda rolled down the window. Barry's stupid frogs were sitting next to her. "There's no room in here," she said.

"Yes there is. I can sit where the frogs are."

"No you can't, you'll squash them. You can

go in the back if you want to come," Wanda answered.

"You must be joking," I told her.

"Minty, is that you?" I heard Uncle Drac's voice coming from the broom closet. "Minty, have you found Big Bat? *Minty?*"

I opened the back door of the van and jumped in. I soon wished I hadn't. The smell was *disgusting*.

~4~
THE MUSHROOM FARM

It was totally horrible in the back of Uncle Drac's van.

The trouble was, Barry and Wanda had shoveled up the wrong kind of bat poo. Uncle Drac always uses the old dry stuff, but they had put new stuff in the sacks. Which is not nice.

The even worse trouble was that Barry is not a good driver. He doesn't like other cars,

and every time he sees one he slams on the brakes. Or speeds up really fast to get away from it. In about two seconds flat, I felt very sick. I leaned against the yucky, squidgy sacks and groaned—and one of the squidgy sacks poked me in the ribs.

"Ow!" I yelled. I was so surprised that I jumped up and hit my head on the roof.

"Ouch!"

So I sat down fast and landed on the sack, which squeaked loudly. Just then the van went around a corner really fast and all the sacks slid over to the side, taking me with them. The pokey sack tipped over and spilled bat poo out all over the floor. It spilled out something else, too—Big Bat.

Big Bat is like Uncle Drac, which is why they get along so well. He is a grumpy old bat

who does not like being messed up—and seeing as Big Bat had recently been messed up big-time, I left him alone. He shook out his wings and then waddled over to the farthest corner of the van, hunched himself up, and looked mad. I understood how he felt.

I was really glad that I had found Big Bat. Just as I was thinking how pleased Uncle Drac would be, Barry slammed on the brakes and the van skidded to a halt. Big Bat, me, and all the sacks slid up to the front of the van. We had arrived at the mushroom farm.

Barry opened the doors and I fell out, gasping for fresh air.

"You've made an awful mess in there," Wanda said disapprovingly as I staggered to a patch of grass and threw myself to the ground.

"Me?" I wheezed. "*I've* made a mess?"

But Wanda, who is *meant* to be my best friend, showed no sympathy for the fact that I was possibly breathing my last breath. She just stomped off and went to help Barry get the sacks out of the van. Then Barry started shoveling all the poo back into the spilled sack—and I remembered Big Bat, who was sulking in the corner of the van.

The back of that van was the last place I wanted to be, but I got in and rescued Big Bat just as Barry was about to shovel him back into the sack. Then I took Big Bat out and put him somewhere he would be safe—I hung him from the rearview mirror. The frogs did not look pleased.

The mushroom farm was a weird place— it looked like a load of old ruins with a few ramshackle sheds in the middle where the mushrooms lived. There was no one about. It was a bit creepy.

"You're looking very pale, Araminta," said Barry, who is a thoughtful person, unlike his daughter. "Why don't you and Wanda go and take a run on the beach while I go and find Old Morris."

The lane from the mushroom farm led to

a low cliff. Wanda and I climbed down some old wooden steps and ran onto the beach. The tide was far out, and there was lots of wet sand to throw at Wanda. She soon got tired of that, though, and went off to look at the caves at the foot of the cliffs.

There is an old story that they are smugglers' caves and that one of them leads to our house. Once I asked Aunt Tabby if that was true, but she just said that you shouldn't believe everything you hear and why would smugglers want to come all the way to *our* house when there are plenty of houses nearer the beach? Why smugglers would want to come to a house with Aunt Tabby in it was more to the point, I thought. They would be just asking for trouble.

Wanda had disappeared into a small cave.

I waited for her to come out, but she didn't. It was boring on the beach on my own, so after a while I went to see what she was doing.

The cave was very narrow and smelled like seaweed. It had a sandy floor and a high, rocky roof. I looked around for Wanda, but she wasn't there. I thought maybe she was hiding and planning to jump out at me, but I couldn't see anywhere to hide.

"Wanda!" I called out. "Hey, Wan-*da*."

"Wanda Wanda Wanda Wan-*da*," echoed back at me.

I walked farther into the cave and switched on my flashlight (Uncle Drac gave me a key ring flashlight for my birthday, and I always carry it just in case). I thought maybe Wanda was lurking somewhere in the shadows. Wanda does that sometimes because she thinks it's funny—which it is not—so I shone the flashlight everywhere. But there was no sign of Wanda, and soon I had reached the end of the cave. Where was she?

"Boo!" yelled Wanda. She suddenly jumped right out in front of me. "Ha-ha, got you, got you!"

"Don't *do* that," I told her. "Where *were* you?"

Wanda looked really pleased with herself. "I was up there," she said, pointing up to the ceiling of the cave.

"Don't be silly, Wanda. How could you get up there?"

"Come on, I'll show you," she said, switching on *her* flashlight. Wanda is such a copycat sometimes.

I had been so busy expecting Wanda to jump out at me that I had not noticed some narrow steps cut into the wall of the cave. I followed Wanda up to a small ledge at the top. There was just about enough room for us both, but most of it was taken up by a massive pile of rocks that reached right up to the roof of the cave.

Wanda was really excited. "Look what I've found," she said. She shone her flashlight through a narrow chink in the rocks, and I peered in. At first I couldn't see what Wanda was on about, but then, as she wiggled the flashlight beam around, I could see the light glinting off some metal.

"It's a sword," said Wanda.

"How do you know?" I asked.

"I've been looking at it forever. I'm *sure* it

is. Go on, take another look."

"Well, how can I when you're stepping on my foot?" I told her. Wanda has surprisingly big feet for such a short person, and she wears big boots, too.

Wanda got off my foot, and I looked again. I didn't want to admit it, but I thought Wanda was right. On the other side of the pile of rocks, I could see a small, round grotto. And in the middle of its sandy floor lay a sword. A really big, serious-looking sword.

"It would make a great five-hundredth birthday present for Sir Horace," said Wanda.

Well, I had to admit that Wanda was right about that, too.

"It would if we could get hold of it," I said. "But there is no way we can squeeze through those rocks."

"No, I suppose not." Wanda sounded disappointed. "Anyway, we ought to go now; Dad will be wondering where we are."

I was thinking about the sword and Sir Horace's birthday all the way back to the mushroom farm. And just before we got back to the van, I said to Wanda, "I know how we can get that sword for Sir Horace."

"*How?*" asked Wanda.

"I'll tell you later," I said. "I have a Plan."

OLD MORRIS

My Plan went right out of my head when we got back to the mushroom farm.

As we reached the gate, we heard someone shouting, and it wasn't Barry. Then we saw Barry being pushed out of the mushroom shed by a tall, thin man with a ponytail and a very loud voice—Morris FitzMaurice, who runs the mushroom farm, or Old Morris, as Uncle Drac calls him.

"Look here," Old Morris was yelling, "I'm usin' nice clean chemicals now, delivered in nice clean sacks at a decent time of day. You can tell that creepy Drac bloke once and for all that I don't want no more of his disgustin' bat stuff. Got that?"

"But—" Barry tried to get a word in, but the ponytail man still had a lot more to say.

"I dunno what he thinks he's doin'— comin' 'round with them sacks in the middle of the night, wakin' us all up, tellin' me how to manage my mushrooms and takin' *no* notice when I tell him I don't want no more of this stuff. Well, I'm tellin' *you* I've had enough of it. Got that?"

"Er, yes," said Barry, "I think I have."

"Good," snapped the ponytail man. "An' you can take them smelly sacks back with you an' all." With that, he stomped back inside the mushroom shed and slammed the door.

Barry began dragging the sacks back to the van. He looked very annoyed.

On the way home, I sat in the front of the van as I *totally* refused to go back with all those sacks. It was not a fun journey. One of Barry's frogs was missing, and Big Bat suddenly looked a lot fatter.

"I'm sure I had five frogs this morning," said Barry.

"Yes, Dad, you did." Wanda glared at me like it was *my* fault. All the way home, Big Bat swung from the rearview mirror, and every time Barry looked in the mirror, Big Bat glared at *him*. Just like Uncle Drac does.

"What is Drac going to say?" muttered Barry as he swerved around a corner and Big

Bat hit his head on the windshield.

"Quite a lot, I expect," I said.

"He'll blame me," said Barry.

"Yes, he will," I agreed.

"He'll say it was all my fault because I didn't deliver it last night."

"Yes," I said, "he will."

Barry didn't say anything for the rest of the ride.

When we got home, Barry parked the van at the front of the house so that Uncle Drac wouldn't hear it. I unhooked Big Bat from the mirror. I was looking forward to giving him to Uncle Drac. But I wasn't looking forward to Uncle Drac finding out what Old Morris had said.

"Are you going to tell Uncle Drac what

happened?" I asked Barry, who had his head stuck under the seat. He was looking for his frog.

Barry mumbled something.

"You'll have to tell him sometime, Dad," said Wanda.

Barry came up for air. "Later," he said. "I'll tell him later, when he feels better."

"You mean when *you* feel better," Wanda said.

Barry sighed. He took off his hat and clicked his fingers. All the frogs that had not been eaten by Big Bat jumped on top of his head. Then Barry put his hat back on and went to get the sacks out of the van.

I crept up to the broom closet door and opened it just a little bit. Then I threw Big Bat in. Bats don't mind being thrown. They just fly wherever they want to go, which is exactly what Big Bat did. He flew into the corner

where Sir Horace was hiding and settled on the top of an old coat.

"Big Bat—oh, *Big Bat!*" gasped Uncle Drac. He sounded really happy. I peered around the door, and Uncle Drac spotted me.

"Minty." He smiled. "I *knew* you'd find Big Bat. Where was he?"

"In a sack—I mean, in a safe place, Uncle Drac. He was fine. Really fine." Uncle Drac looked so pleased that I did not want to spoil things by mentioning the mushroom farm. So I didn't. But the trouble was, Uncle Drac mentioned it.

"Did Barry take the bat poo to the mushroom farm?" Uncle Drac picked up his weird green knitting.

"Yes, he did, Uncle Drac. That's a very nice scarf you're knitting."

"Oh, do you really think so, Minty? And Barry made sure he gave the bat poo *personally* to Old Morris, did he?"

"Oh, yes, he certainly saw him personally, Uncle Drac. No doubt about that. Your scarf is quite long now, isn't it?"

"Yes, I'll need some more yarn soon. Did Old Morris mind about the bat poo being late, Minty?"

"I'll go and find you some more yarn, Uncle Drac. Back in a minute."

Phew. I got out of the broom closet fast and bumped straight into Wanda.

"Have you told him?" she whispered.

"No. Barry can tell him. Anyway, we've got things to do. I've got a Plan—remember?"

Wanda did not look as impressed as she should have.

"What *kind* of Plan?" she asked suspiciously.

~6~

STRING

String is very important when you are going to explore a secret passage. The trouble was, I couldn't find any. I had everything else ready from my Secret Passage Kit—my big flashlight, cheese and onion chips, and a can of Coke—but the string was gone. I figured Aunt Tabby had taken it.

Wanda kept asking me irritating questions about my Plan, but I said there was no point

telling her anything, as it wasn't going to happen unless we found some string—and lots of it. So Wanda went to find some, and I sat on the attic stairs and thought through my Plan.

It was a really brilliant Plan, but then my Plans always are. We were going to go and get the sword in the grotto and give it to Sir Horace for his birthday. And how were we going to do that? Yes—you've guessed it. We would get to the grotto through the smugglers' secret passage. How about that for a great idea?

The more I thought about it, the more sure I was that Aunt Tabby was wrong about smugglers not wanting to come to our house. It was really a great house for smugglers—lots of rooms to hide stuff in, and far enough away from the sea so that no one would suspect anything. When I had first discovered the secret passage to Sir Horace's room, I had followed it all the way down to behind the boiler room in the basement. Edmund lives in that part of the passage. I hadn't gone any farther, but I could see that it carried on. And where else would it go but to the grotto? It was obvious, really.

Then Wanda turned up with a huge ball of green string. "Mom let me borrow this from her prizewinning string collection," she said. "She wants it back, though."

I smiled. Wanda can be quite nice at times.

"*Now* will you tell me your Plan?" she said.

Soon we were climbing down the rickety old ladder that leads from Sir Horace's room.

Wanda didn't like it one bit. She was saying stuff like, "But horrible things might be living down there" and "How do you know it leads to the grotto?" which I was answering very patiently, considering that every time she said something the ladder wobbled, and I was holding on to it with only one hand, since I was the one with the flashlight.

But when we were halfway down

the ladder, Wanda suddenly stopped and wailed, "Suppose we get lost and we never find our way out again and we spend the rest of our lives just wandering around in the dark *forever?*" And the ladder shook so much that I practically fell off.

"Oh, *be quiet*, Wanda," I said.

She didn't say anything else.

Soon we got to the bottom of the ladder, which I was really pleased about, but Wanda still looked miserable.

"Look, Wanda," I said very patiently. "We tied the end of the green string to the secret door, didn't we?"

Wanda nodded.

"And you've got the string, haven't you?"

Wanda nodded again.

"So all we have to do is unwind your

mom's green string as we go until we get to the grotto. Then we just pick up the sword and follow the string home again. Easy peasy. There's no *way* we can get lost, is there?"

"I suppose not," said Wanda. And then she thought for a bit. "Unless something *eats* the string."

"Don't be silly, Wanda."

"And if something started to eat the string, then the string would lead it straight to us and it would eat us, too!" Wanda wailed.

"Oh, *shut up*, Wanda."

Now the secret passage was more like a regular tunnel. The walls were made of bricks, and the ceiling was tall enough for Wanda and me to stand up easily. It was arched and made of brick, too. The floor was quite hard, like earth, and was covered with sand. It was pretty warm down there because we were getting close to where the passage runs behind the boiler room. I was looking out for Edmund, but it was Wanda who saw him first.

"Hello, Edmund," said Wanda. Edmund floated around the corner and came toward us. Unlike Sir Horace, who just looks like an old suit of armor, Edmund looks like a real ghost. He is a boy of about ten, I guess, but he is an almost transparent boy with a greenish glow around him. He has a pudding-bowl haircut, wears a medieval tunic with a long hood, and carries a really neat dagger in his belt.

"Good Day, Wanda. Good Day, Araminta," said Edmund in his funny old-fashioned accent. The hair on the back of my neck stood up, like it always does when Edmund speaks. His voice has a hollow sound to it, and it's hard to tell where it is coming from.

"Hello, Edmund," said Wanda.

Edmund was floating around in front of us in a rather annoying fashion and was generally getting in the way. I could see what an irritating boy he must have once been.

"Excuse me, Edmund," I said, "we'd like to get past. Do you mind moving out of the way? We don't want to walk through you."

"Where are you going?" asked Edmund.

I was about to tell him it was none of his business, but Wanda piped up and said, "We're going to the smugglers' grotto to get the sword. You can come too if you want, Edmund."

"No he can't," I told Wanda. "We're in a hurry, and Edmund only floats very slowly." Besides that, considering he's a ghost, Edmund is boring and a bit of a goody-goody, but I was too polite to say that.

"You must go back. You may not come any closer," said Edmund in his spooky voice.

"Don't be silly," I told him, and I tried to push him out of the way.

It was *horrible*. My hand went right through him and out the other side. Suddenly I felt frozen. I shivered so hard that my teeth chattered, and when I snatched my arm back all the hairs on it were *covered in ice*.

"Arrgh!" I screamed.

"What?" squeaked Wanda, looking scared. "What is it?"

"It's Edmund. He's freezing. It's horrible.

Brrr." I shivered again. I just couldn't help it.

When Wanda saw all the icicles on my arm, her eyes opened so wide that I thought they might fall out. Any minute now, I thought, Wanda is going to panic big-time.

But she didn't. She put her hand in her pocket and took something out and then really fast, like a flash of light, she threw a shower of sparkly dust over Edmund. *Whhoooosh.*

The dust settled over him like snow. Edmund looked confused for a moment, then he yawned, lay down on the sandy floor, and went to sleep. I was impressed.

"What was *that?*" I asked Wanda.

"Soporific Snow," she said. "Dad gave me some from his magic bag. Good, isn't it?"

"Good? It's *amazing.* Wow." Barry is a con-jurer, and sometimes he does tricks for us, but I had never seen one as good as this.

"Come on then," said Wanda, "we'd better get going." And she strode off, unwinding the ball of green string as she went.

"Hey, Wanda," I yelled, "wait for me!"

~7~
THE SECRET TUNNEL

Not long after we had got past Edmund, we noticed that the air was different— it felt cold and damp and it smelled of earth. The walls of the secret tunnel changed too— now they were roughly cut rock. The light from my flashlight shone off the damp rocks and we knew that we were no longer inside the house. We were under the ground—this was the real thing.

The tunnel was quite wide, and Wanda and I walked along side by side. After a while Wanda whispered, "How far down do you think we are?"

"I don't know," I whispered back. And then I whispered, "Why are we whispering?"

"Because it's scary," whispered Wanda.

"No it's not," I said really loudly, and my voice sounded hollow like Edmund's. Well, maybe it was a *bit* scary.

Wanda was good with the string. She kept unwinding it as we went, and when I looked back, I could see it stretching along the tunnel. It was nice to think that the end of the string was still there, tied to the secret door under the attic stairs.

We had walked for about half an hour, and I reckoned we were probably almost underneath the mushroom farm, when we went around a corner and Wanda suddenly said, "Which way do we go *now*?"

In front of us, the secret tunnel split off into two smaller tunnels. They both looked narrow and they both looked dark. I didn't like the look of either of them.

"I don't know," I said. "Do you want some chips?"

Cheese and onion potato chips help you think. I am sure of that, because after we had finished them, we knew what we had to do.

"Right," I said.

"Left," said Wanda.

So we did rock, paper, scissors—best of three—and Wanda won. Then we did best of five and I won. So we went right.

Big mistake.

It was okay to begin with. Kind of. The tunnel I had chosen smelled funny. It reminded me of something, but I couldn't think what. And just as I was about to remember what it smelled of, Wanda said, "*Now* which way?" as if it was *my* fault that the tunnel had split up again—this time into three ways.

"Middle one," I said.

"Why?" asked Wanda.

"Why not?" I said. "It doesn't matter if it's not right. We can always find our way back along the string and try the other one."

Wanda wasn't happy. "We could be here for days doing that," she said. "And we haven't got much more string left."

We set off down the middle tunnel, which was an okay tunnel, as tunnels go, but still smelled funny—and then suddenly Wanda screamed.

"Arrgh!"

I dropped my flashlight.

"Oh, yuck. Oh, *errgh*." Wanda was hopping

about like something had bitten her.

"Wh-what is it?"

"I—I stepped on a *dead body*. . . ." Wanda squeaked. "I-it was all squashy a-and horrible. My foot went right through it." She shivered and grabbed hold of me. "I want to go home," she whispered.

Well, that made two of us.

I went to pick up my flashlight, and Wanda screamed again.

"Everything's turned white," she yelled. "*Look*. . . ."

I didn't want to look, but I did. The flashlight shone along the ground, lighting up the floor of the tunnel. It was the weirdest thing I have ever seen—a kind of knobbly white carpet stretched out in front of us.

"Mushrooms. You only stepped on a *mush-room*," I told Wanda, annoyed.

Wanda looked down at her feet. "Oh," she said. Then she said, "Well, it was a giant mushroom, actually, Araminta. Look— they're huge. You try stepping on a whole heap of monster mushrooms in a horrible, dark, smelly tunnel and see what *you* feel like."

"I just did," I told Wanda, "and I felt fine. And I didn't go screaming in someone's ear, nearly making them deaf, either."

Wanda didn't reply. I thought maybe I should try to cheer her up a bit, so I said, "Well, at least we know where we are now."

"No we don't," said Wanda gloomily.

"Yes we do. These mushrooms must have escaped from the mushroom farm. I bet we are underneath it right now. Which means we are nearly there. Come *on*, Wanda. It will all be worth it when we find the sword."

"*If* we find the sword," Wanda muttered.

We didn't say much after that except for, "left," "right," "left—no, right," and "oh, I don't care, you choose." The trouble was, the tunnel just kept splitting off into different directions, and we had no idea which one would take us to the cave. It was like being in a maze—a horrible mushroom maze, as the whole time we were stepping on mushrooms. At first I felt sorry for them getting squashed, but after a while they just got annoying. They were really slippery, too.

We kept on hoping that any minute we would find the grotto with the sword in it. But we didn't. All we kept finding was the green string, so we knew we were back to where we had been before. Again.

After a while Wanda said, "It's no good. We're just going around in circles."

For once she was right.

~8~

THE PORTCULLIS

Wanda was not good at going around in circles. She did not take it well.

"All right, Wanda," I said. "If we haven't found the sword in five minutes' time, we'll go home."

"Promise?" asked Wanda.

"Promise," I said. I knew we'd have to go home soon anyway, since our string was nearly finished.

Wanda spent the next four minutes and forty seconds staring at her watch and counting the seconds in a loud voice. It was very annoying, especially as I still really wanted to find the sword and give it to Sir Horace for his birthday.

We were walking down a steep slope. The mushrooms had disappeared, and I knew we had not been here before. Wanda was so busy staring at her watch that she did not notice when suddenly we turned a corner and there it was—the little round grotto with the sandy floor and the sword lying there in the middle of it, just waiting for us, like I had known it would be.

Incredible!

"Wanda," I said, "look!"

But Wanda was still droning on, "Two

hundred and seventy-eight seconds . . . two
hundred and seventy-nine seconds . . . two
hundred and—"

"Wan-*da*," I yelled. "We've *found* it!"

At last Wanda stopped counting and
looked up. "Wow . . ." She whistled under her
breath. Wanda was about to rush in when
suddenly I remembered what it said in my
Secret Tunnel Handy Hint Handbook.

Handy Hint #3: Watch out for traps,
particularly at the beginning and end of a
tunnel. How often has an intrepid tunneler
battled through the most secret of tunnels
only to come to grief in a cunning trap at
the end of her journey? Alas, far too often,
as we at the *Secret Tunnel Handy Hint
Handbook* know to our cost.

"Stop!" I yelled to Wanda—and just in time. Because right above our heads, where the secret tunnel went into the cave, I could see five horrible metal spikes pointing down at us.

Wanda stopped dead in her tracks. "What are you shouting about now?" she asked grumpily. "I thought you wanted to get the sword. It's stupid to stop now when all we have to do is just—"

"Wan-daaa." I sighed very patiently. "Just look up, will you?"

Wanda looked up. "Oh," she said. "What is it?"

"It's a trap," I told her. "A horrible trap."

Wanda stared at the spikes for a bit, then she said, "No it's not. It's a portcullis." Miss Know-it-all Wanda Wizzard folded her

arms and looked smug.

"I know that," I said. "I didn't say it *wasn't* a portcullis. I just said it was a trap. Obviously it is a portcullis trap."

"Obviously," said Miss Smug Pants.

"What we have to do," I told her, "is make sure there aren't any trip wires."

Wanda looked worried. "Why?" she asked.

"Because if there is a trip wire and we trip over it, then the portcullis will come crashing down on top of our heads, that's why."

Wanda shuddered. "That's *horrible*," she said.

I shrugged. "Stuff like that happens all the time in secret tunnels."

"Well, you never told me that when you were trying to get me to come with you," said

Wanda, staring up at the sharp spikes.

"You never asked," I told her. I crouched down and shone my flashlight along the ground, which was covered in thick sand.

"It's okay," I said. "I can't see a trip wire or anything, so I guess we're safe."

I don't think Wanda believed me. She got down on her hands and knees and had a real good look too. "I guess it's okay. . . ." she muttered.

"Do you want to go first?" I offered. I was being polite, as Aunt Tabby is always telling me not to rush in front of people.

Wanda gave me a funny look and said, "No thank you, Araminta. We'll go together." She grabbed hold of my hand and yelled, "One . . . two . . . three . . . Go!"

So we went. We shot under the portcullis like a couple of bats out of a sack and *nothing happened*. The horrible spikes stayed just where they were, and there we were—in the grotto at last.

"Yes!" I grinned at Wanda. "We did it!"

Wanda ran around the cave, kicking up the sand and jumping about, yelling, "We did it, we did it. Yaay!" I think she was pleased too.

And then there was a horrible clang and a huge thud. The grotto shook like an earthquake had struck. But it was a whole heap worse than an earthquake.

It was the portcullis trap—it had come crashing down. Now a massive iron grille barred our way home.

Wanda and I stared at it. Even Wanda didn't say anything for a while. And then, when she did say something, her voice sounded all squeaky and trembling.

"We're *trapped*," she said.

Wanda was right. Again.

THE GROTTO

Wanda did not take too well to being trapped in the grotto, either. In fact, she took it even worse than she'd taken going around in circles. I told her that it was no good jumping up and down and yelling; we had to try and get out.

First we tried to lift up the portcullis, but it weighed a ton. It didn't budge one little bit. We kept on trying, but I could tell there

was no way we could move it in a million years.

"And there's no point shouting 'One, two, three . . . *heave*' in my ear over and over again," I told Wanda. "It's not going to help if I go deaf as well."

After that we tried to dig down below the portcullis. The sand was soft, and I thought that maybe we could squeeze out underneath, but it was no good. There was rock below the sand, and also a thick metal plate, which I guessed was part of the portcullis trap.

"Come on, Wanda," I said. "We've *got* to lift up that portcullis."

But it wouldn't shift. Then we tried stupid things that we knew wouldn't work, but we had to do them just in case. We tried to squeeze underneath, but we couldn't fit. Wanda tried wriggling through the gaps between the bars, as she is smaller than I am, but she nearly got her head stuck. We even used the sword to try to lever up the metal plate under the sand. But the portcullis stayed right where it was, blocking our way home.

Wanda acted a bit strange after that. She started shaking the bars and yelling for help. I didn't see the point, so I went and sat down beside the sword and tried to think. But however hard I tried, I couldn't think of anything. And soon all I could think was, "I wish Wanda would stop *yelling*."

"Shut up, Wanda," I said.

"Shut up yourself," said Wanda. She sounded really annoyed, but underneath I could tell she was as scared as I was. When I'm scared I get very quiet, but when Wanda is scared she just goes bananas.

"Do you want a cheese and onion chip?" I asked.

"No. I'm not hungry," she said. But she stopped yelling and came and sat down beside me.

I felt much better after I had eaten my potato chips. I decided I might as well have a look at the sword, seeing as we had come all this way to find it. You could tell that it had once been a really great sword. The handle had some nice patterns on it, and there were some lumpy bits under all the dirt and rust flakes that looked like they might be jewels. But I had to admit that my first impression of it had been better, because in fact it now looked like a piece of old junk. It was the kind of thing that Aunt Tabby would bring back from a garage sale and Uncle Drac would sigh and ask why on earth did we need *more* garbage. But I still knew it was the perfect birthday present for Sir Horace.

"It's great, isn't it?" I said. "Sir Horace is going to love this; I know he will."

"If he ever gets to see it," muttered Wanda,

"which he won't. Because tomorrow on his birthday, we'll still be stuck here. And the next day. And the day after that. We're *always* going to be stuck here. I'm never going to see Mom and Dad again, and you're never going to see your aunt Tabby or uncle Drac again— never mind Sir Stupid Horace."

"Stop it, Wanda," I said. "Just stop it *right now*. We are going to get out of here. There is always more than one way out of a secret tunnel."

"There used to be," said Wanda, pointing to the pile of rocks that blocked off the grotto from the cave outside, "but there isn't anymore."

We went over to the rock pile anyway. I shone the flashlight everywhere, hoping to see a gap that we could squeeze through, but there was nothing. Nothing but horrible, heavy rocks.

Wanda peered through a tiny gap between two rocks. "This is where I looked through from the other side," she said. "Maybe if we shine the flashlight through here, some people on the beach might see it. Or there might be someone in the cave exploring."

Well, it was worth a try. I didn't mention the fact that you can't see the end of the cave from the beach, or that it must be getting late by now and everyone would be going home. I just gave Wanda the flashlight.

She shone it through the gap. "Coo-*eee*," she called out, sounding just like Brenda does when she calls her cat. "Is anybody there?" Wanda put her ear to the gap and listened hard.

"Can you hear something?" I whispered.

"Shh . . . yes . . . yes I can."

.   I felt really excited. How lucky was *that*, someone being in the cave just at that moment? "What— *what* can you hear, Wanda?" I asked. "Tell me!"

Wanda stood up and gave me back the flashlight. She had a

really weird look on her face. "I can hear the sea," she said. "It's inside the cave."

I didn't believe Wanda at first. I thought she was just doing another Wanda windup. But this time she was dead calm.

"What do you mean, it's inside the cave?" I asked. "The sea doesn't come inside the cave. You saw where it was this morning. It was miles away. I've never seen it so far away."

"Then it was low tide," muttered Wanda. "Now it's high tide."

"So?" I asked. I wasn't really sure what Wanda meant, as I hadn't been to the beach very much. Aunt Tabby doesn't like the way the sand gets inside her shoes, and Uncle Drac won't go out in the sun. In fact, until Wanda came to live with us I had never been to the beach.

"So—the sea was really far out this morning, wasn't it?" said Wanda. I nodded. "And when it goes far out, that means it's a really *low* tide. Okay? But it also means that when it comes in, like it's doing now, it will be a really *high* tide."

I didn't like the sound of this. "How high?" I asked.

"I don't know," said Wanda. "But it's not high tide until seven o'clock. That's when Mom was going down for her swim."

I looked at my watch. It said half past five. One and a half hours still to go.

"Give me the flashlight," I said. "I want to see the water inside the cave."

I found the gap in the rocks and shone the flashlight through. At first I couldn't see anything at all, but I kept the flashlight very still and stared until my eyes got used to it.

"Can you see anything?" Wanda asked in a hoarse whisper.

"There's something moving . . . the light . . . it's reflecting off something. . . ."

"Water," said Wanda glumly.

"Yes," I said. "Waves."

"Waves," Wanda repeated in a flat voice.

"Only little waves," I said, trying to cheer her up.

Wanda didn't say anything.

I didn't see the point of just staring at the water, waiting for it to come closer. It was still quite a few feet away, and I didn't totally believe what Wanda had said about high tide—Wanda can get a bit worked up about things. So I sat down on the sand to think.

"That's why the sand is damp," Wanda said, throwing herself down beside me.

"What's why the sand is damp?"

Wanda laughed in a funny way that I didn't like. "Because at the last high tide, the sea came in here."

"You don't know that," I told her. She grabbed the flashlight and shone it around the walls of the grotto like she was looking for something. And then she found it.

"Seaweed," she said, waving the light over a piece of shiny green stuff stuck on the ceiling. "And it's still wet."

I tried to remember what Uncle Drac always says about not panicking, but I couldn't. Even Uncle Drac might panic a bit just now.

I didn't say anything for a while, and then

Wanda—being
her usual cheery
self—said,
"Araminta . . ."

"What?"

"Can you swim?"

"No. Can you?"

"Yes . . . with arm floats."

"Don't suppose you brought them with
you?"

"No . . ."

There didn't seem much else to
talk about after that.

~10~

RINSE CYCLE

The sea kept on coming, and the sound of the waves washing against the walls of the cave outside got louder. Soon I could smell the sea in the air.

I looked at the green string, which had ended just as we reached the grotto. It lay on the sand beside my backpack, and I thought of the other end tied to the secret door underneath the attic stairs. More than anything I

wished I was at *that* end of the string. And then—

I saw it *move*.

I didn't believe it. And then it moved again.

Wanda saw it too. "Something's eating the string," she whispered. "And soon it will come and eat *us*."

"Don't be silly, Wanda. How will it get through the portcullis?"

"It probably set the portcullis trap in the

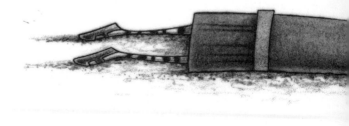

first place," said Wanda. "It will just press a button or something and—"

"Stop it, Wanda!" I put my fingers in my ears.

Suddenly there was a huge tug on the string, and it jumped underneath the portcullis.

"Get it, get it!" yelled Wanda. I dived to grab it, but it was too late—the end was just out of reach. Wanda and I watched the green string move jerkily along the tunnel until it

disappeared around the corner.

"Now we'll never find our way home," I mumbled, "even if we do get through the portcullis trap."

"Which we won't," said Wanda.

We could hear the sea getting even closer. There was a kind of swishing sound as the water gushed into the narrow cave outside and swirled around the rocks, and then a sucking sound as the water washed out again, and then another *swishhhh* . . . and then it happened.

The sea poured in. It came in through the tiny gaps in the pile of rocks like water through a cheese grater. At first all it did was sink into the sand and disappear, but it was not long before there was a pool of water in the sand that didn't go away. And every time a wave threw itself against the rocks, more water poured in and the pool got deeper. The noise was horrible too. Now I knew how Brenda's cat, Pusskins, must have felt the day Aunt Tabby ran the rinse cycle while it was asleep in the washing machine. I decided I would never, ever laugh at Brenda's cat again. If I ever *saw* Brenda's cat again...

The rinse cycle in the grotto just carried on. More and more water was coming in and, although Wanda and I were on the high bit of sand by the portcullis, we knew that it would not be long before the water reached us, too—and then kept going right up to that piece of seaweed way above our heads.

Suddenly there was a massive *thud* against the rocks. A wave of water streamed in and splashed up at us. Wanda screamed and dropped the flashlight. It rolled down the sand toward the water.

"Get it!" I yelled. "Quick!"

We both dived after it. I crashed into Wanda and fell into the water. Wanda yelled and missed the flashlight, which rolled into the pool.

Any other time I would have thought how pretty it looked. It lit up the water as it sank, and the whole grotto turned a bluey-green. We watched as the light dropped slowly down and came to rest on the sand at the bottom of the pool.

And then it went out. And everything went black.

Wanda grabbed hold of me so hard that it hurt. "It's dark," she whispered. "I—I don't like the dark."

It wasn't the dark I minded; it was the water. But I didn't say that. I just said, "I-it's okay. I've got my key ring flashlight." I pulled it out of my pocket and pressed the button. But it didn't work. It was wet.

"Where's yours?" I asked Wanda.

She fumbled through her pockets for ages, and then she said, "It's not here. I think I left it in the cave. . . ."

"Never mind," I said. "There must be some light getting in through the gaps in the rocks. Just wait until your eyes get used to it."

But our eyes didn't get used to it.

It was horrible being in the dark. Really horrible. We couldn't see the water anymore, so we didn't know how fast it was coming up toward us, and I kept thinking we were about to get drowned. I opened my eyes so wide that they felt cold around the edges, but it made no difference. I could see nothing at all. It was completely, totally dark.

Another rush of water poured between the rocks, and I felt the spray in my face as it splashed in.

"At least Pusskins could *see* something," I said to Wanda. "Aunt Tabby always leaves the light on in the laundry room."

"What are you talking about?" gasped Wanda.

"Nothing," I said. "Move back a bit, Wanda, my feet are in the water."

"I can't," she said. "There's no room. I'm stuck right against the portcullis already."

"Well, start climbing it then," I told her. "My feet are soaked. I hate having wet socks."

The portcullis was quite easy to climb, even in the dark. I hung the sword onto one of the bars and followed Wanda up until we both were as high as we could get. The metal was cold and sharp, but I didn't care. At least we were out of the water. But for how long?

We didn't say much after that. The waves

kept on pounding outside on the rocks, then pouring into the grotto. The water was right up to our knees and there was no way we could climb any higher when suddenly Wanda said, "A light! I can see a light in the tunnel. Look, *look*!"

I nearly fell off the portcullis. Wanda was right. At the far end of the mushroom tunnel was a very faint greenish glow. *And it was coming toward us.*

DEEP WATER

I just knew it had to be good old Aunt Tabby. It was Aunt Tabby who had been pulling the string, not some horrible monster, and she was coming to rescue us.

"Aunt Tabby, Aunt Tabby!" I shouted. "We're here!"

"Help, help!" Wanda yelled, just to make sure.

But there was no reply.

"It might be Dad," said Wanda. "Dad, Dad—it's *me*. I'm here, Dad!"

"I'm here too," I told Wanda. "Don't forget about *me*."

"Ha!" Wanda gave a funny kind of laugh. I ignored her and just kept on watching the green light flickering at the far end of the tunnel. It was moving slowly, but it was definitely coming down toward us.

Wanda said nervously, "It's a weird light for a flashlight. It's not very bright, is it?"

I had been thinking that too. "No," I said, "it's not. . . ."

"Dad!" Wanda shouted. *"Dad!"* We listened for Barry's reply, but there was nothing. All we could hear was the *slip* and *slop* of the water washing around us.

"It's not Dad, is it?" Wanda whispered miserably.

"No, it's not," I said. "I think it's—"

"It's the monster, isn't it—the one that ate the string? And now it's going to come and—"

"Shut up, Wanda," I said. "It's not a monster. It's *Edmund*."

The greenish light was floating along the tunnel toward us in just the way that Edmund floats. As it got closer, I could see that it had a definite Edmund shape to it, right down to the silly haircut.

"It *is*," gasped Wanda. "It's Edmund. He's come to rescue us!"

"Wanda," I said, "how exactly do you expect a weedy little ghost like Edmund to rescue us? Or even a big strong ghost? No ghost can lift up the portcullis and let us out, can it?"

But Wanda wasn't listening. "Edmund, Edmund, help! We're trapped! Help, *help!*" she yelled.

Edmund's hollow, ghostly voice came echoing along the tunnel. **"Waaan-da,"** he called out. **"Aramin-ta."**

I shivered. Maybe it was the creepy sound of Edmund's voice in the dark, maybe it was the weird green light, or maybe it was the really cold water, which was splashing up to our waists by now—but I started to shiver and I just couldn't stop.

Edmund floated up to the portcullis and stared at us.

"There's no need to gape like we're in a zoo or something," I told him. "We've got to get out of here. W-we're going to drown if we don't."

"I know . . ." said Edmund in his hollow voice.

"Well, thanks a lot, Edmund," I snapped at him. "We feel a whole lot better now."

"I know . . ." said Edmund, "because I drowned here. With Sir Horace . . ."

"Drowned?" Wanda squeaked.

"Drowned," Edmund repeated gloomily.

I must say I didn't think Edmund was exactly being helpful just then.

"Edmund," I said, "will you please go back as fast as you can to the house and tell Aunt Tabby where we are? She'll know what to do. Please. *Hurry*."

"It is too late to return to the house," said Edmund.

"What are we going to *doooo*?" Wanda wailed.

"Be quiet, Wanda."

"Do not fret, Wanda," said Edmund. **"We will take the other way out. There is just enough time before the water becomes too deep."** Edmund floated through the portcullis easily, as if it wasn't there, and hovered beside us, lighting up the horrible little grotto with his ghostly glow.

Now I was glad that we hadn't had our flashlights for a while, because what we saw was scary—the grotto was almost full of dark, deep water. And every time a wave hit the rocks, more sea swirled in and the water rose a little bit more. I looked up at Wanda's piece of seaweed on the ceiling, and I knew she had been right. The water was just going to keep on rising. Right to the top . . .

"**Follow me.**" Edmund's voice interrupted my thoughts, which was a good thing, as I had been about to throw a Wanda-sized panic. He floated away toward the pile of rocks where the sea was coming in.

Wanda wailed, "We can't follow you. We'll *drown*."

I was thinking the same thing. I was also thinking, how come Edmund thinks he can rescue *us* when he obviously couldn't rescue himself all those years ago?

Edmund's voice echoed around the cavern. "**The water is not yet too deep, Wanda. You must trust me.**"

"Ooooh!" wailed Wanda.

Edmund came back toward us. Then he started sinking down through the water until he was up to his neck in seawater.

"Don't go, Edmund!" yelled Wanda.

"I am not going, Wanda," he said. **"I am showing you how deep the water is. But soon it will be deeper. You must hurry. You must get down from the portcullis and follow me."**

"Come on, Wanda," I said. "We've got to do this." I started to climb down the portcullis, which was not a nice thing to do, as the water was freezing cold and came to way above my waist. I grabbed hold of the sword and hung on to it to stop myself from falling over.

Wanda hadn't moved. She looked down at me and said, "But I'm shorter than you. It will be almost up to my head."

"All the more reason for getting a move

on," I told her briskly.

"You sound just like Aunt Tabby," she said. But she began to climb down the portcullis and soon, after a bit of squeaking, she was standing next to me.

And then a really big wave came in and knocked her over. Wanda disappeared under the water.

"Blermphh!" Wanda came up for air and waved her arms about like a crazy windmill.

"**Hurry, hurry,**" said Edmund anxiously.

Wanda was still doing her windmill impression, so I grabbed hold of her with my other hand and towed her along behind Edmund until he stopped at the big pile of rocks that blocked the grotto off from the rest of the cave.

Now it was getting really difficult to stand

up, as the water was up to my chin, and it was still coming in. Wanda tried to put her feet down and disappeared right under again. I pulled her up and said, "Just keep on swimming, Wanda."

"B-but I can't swim without arm floats."

"You just have been, in case you hadn't noticed."

Edmund had floated to the top of the pile of rocks. "**Climb up here,**" he said.

"How?" spluttered Wanda.

"Just *do* it, Wanda," I told her. "Just grab hold of a rock and *climb*."

So Wanda did. She heaved herself out of the water and climbed right up. I dragged the sword out of the water and followed her, although I didn't really see the point. We'd looked everywhere for a way out before, and we hadn't see anything.

And then our worst nightmare happened. Edmund disappeared.

"Ed-*mund*," Wanda wailed in the dark.

"Through here, Wanda," came Edmund's hollow voice from the other side of the rocks. And then we saw it. Right at the very top of the rock pile, hidden behind a large flat rock, was the *way out*.

It may have been narrow, and it may have

been full of a weird boy ghost called Edmund, but who cared? All we had to do was squeeze through the gap behind the big flat rock and we would be free.

Which is what we did. And we were. *Free*.

~12~

EDMUND

We may have been free, but we were still stuck. We were now sitting high up on the ledge inside the cave—the same ledge where we had stood that morning and looked down at the sword. But of course the cave was still full of water.

"**You are safe**," said Edmund. "**Now you must wait for the tide to go out.**"

"How long will *that* take?" we both asked.

"It will take two hours and fifteen minutes," said Edmund. "**Farewell, I must be gone.**"

"Gone?" squeaked Wanda. "You can't go and leave us here all alone."

"**But Wanda, you are safe. The sea does not reach up here. All you have to do is wait for the water to recede. I have left my post for too long. I must return to my duties in the tunnel.**"

"What duties in the tunnel?" I asked him, wondering what on earth Edmund had to do that was so important. Polish the dust? Vacuum up the spiders?

"**I guard the way. I must stop anyone from passing from the house and suffering the same fate that Sir Horace and I did so many years ago. But today,**" said Edmund sadly, "**I failed in my task.**"

"No you didn't," I told him. "You came and

saved us. Thank you, Edmund."

"Thank you, Edmund," said Wanda. And then, because she is nosy, Wanda asked, "But what were you and Sir Horace doing in that horrible grotto?"

"We were escaping our enemies, the FitzMaurice family. It was a cowardly attack. There were more than twenty of them and two of us."

"One and a half, more like," I said. "You're only a boy, Edmund. And quite weedy."

"No he's not," said Wanda. "I think he's really strong. What happened then, Edmund?"

"We fled to the grotto beneath Sir Horace's castle. Many years before, Sir Horace had placed a portcullis trap to keep our enemies from the caves under his castle, and he had fashioned a cunning maze to confuse them. But the trap sprung on us, leaving us at the mercy of our pursuers."

"Oh, Edmund, how awful." Wanda sounded thrilled.

"Indeed it was, Wanda. We fought hard but Sir Horace was injured. Then our enemies piled up the rocks and trapped us in the grotto, leaving us at the mercy of the sea."

"Oh, Edmund," breathed Wanda.

Edmund bowed. **"Farewell Wanda. Araminta."** But as he began to disappear, I remembered something I wanted to ask him. Something that had been bugging me ever since he told us that he had drowned in the cave.

"Edmund," I said.

"I must be gone. . . ."

"Edmund—I just want to know—you knew the way out, so why didn't you escape when *you* were trapped?"

"Sir Horace was injured. He could not climb to the top of the rocks," he said. **"And a good and faithful page stays by his master. At all times."**

"Even if he will drown?" I asked.

"He will stay at all times," Edmund repeated

solemnly. And then he was gone.

"Wow . . ." said Wanda after a while. "He's so brave."

I didn't say anything. I tried to imagine what it must have been like all those years ago for Edmund, stuck in that ghastly grotto with Sir Horace and deciding not to escape— but I couldn't even start.

It was dark when Wanda and I at long last got out of the cave. The full moon was rising over the sea and the beach was empty. I was glad, as I didn't want anyone to ask stupid questions about how come we were soaking wet and dragging a great big rusty sword behind us. I had a feeling that once we got home, we were going to be asked enough stupid questions to keep us going for quite a while.

As we walked up the steps from the beach, Wanda suddenly yelled out, "Dad!" and shot off. I slowly dragged the sword up the rest of the steps. I didn't believe that Barry was there. I mean, how would he know where to find us?

But he *was* there!

Good old Barry gave a loud whoop and ran toward us. He scooped Wanda up in his arms and swung her around, then he rushed over to me and did the same.

"You're here!" he gasped. "I don't believe it. You really are here—just like it said."

"Like what said, Dad?" asked Wanda.

"Well, you won't believe this," said Barry with a big grin, "I didn't believe it either, but I knew it was worth a try."

"What was worth a try, Dad?" asked Wanda.

"Well, about half an hour ago, Tabitha found some writing in the coal dust on top of the boiler. Which was odd, as you know how clean Mom keeps the boiler. Anyway, the writing—which was very peculiar and hard to read—said 'W & A Be Upon the Beach.' Tabitha had a screaming fit, as she thought it was a ransom note, but I calmed her down and said I would go and find you. And here you are. . . ." Barry shook his head as though he did not believe it.

Wanda and I were both in the van and Barry was about to drive off when I remembered something. "The sword! We're not going without the sword. Not after all the trouble we've had getting it."

So Barry got out and picked up the sword.

"Where did you find that rusty piece of junk?" he asked as we drove past the mushroom farm and took the road home.

"You don't want to know that," I told him.

"Oh, yes I do," said Barry. "And I can think of a few other people who do, too."

~13~

HAPPY BIRTHDAY

It was fine back home, once the police had gone. Even Aunt Tabby was nice to us, and Uncle Drac was so happy to see us he just couldn't stop smiling.

Aunt Tabby brought in some hot chocolate and everybody sat in the broom closet while Wanda and I told them what had happened. When we got to the bit about the water coming into the grotto, it went very quiet—then

CLANK! Sir Horace lurched out from underneath the pile of coats and everyone yelled in surprise. At the same time the clock in the hall struck midnight. Brenda's cat shot out of the room, and we didn't see it again for a week.

I could tell that Sir Horace was about to start on a long lecture about how we should never have gone down the secret tunnel, how dangerous the grotto was, and generally boring stuff like that—which I knew we would be hearing from Aunt Tabby for months anyway—so I shouted out, "Happy early five-hundredth birthday!" and everyone looked at me like I'd gone crazy.

"Well, it *is* almost his birthday," I told them. "And he's five hundred years old tomorrow. Aren't you, Sir Horace?"

"Yes, unfortunately," Sir Horace boomed. He didn't sound very pleased about it. I didn't know why, because I always love my birthdays.

"Five hundred is very old," said Wanda, trying to cheer him up. "You must be so excited, Sir Horace."

"Not really," he replied gloomily. "Five hundred is indeed very old, Miss Wizzard. It seems so much older than four hundred and ninety-nine."

Well, they both sounded pretty old to me, but I didn't say so. Instead I dragged the sword in and said, "Here's your present, Sir Horace. I'm sorry we didn't have time to wrap it up. Happy Birthday!"

Sir Horace took the sword. He didn't say anything at all. He just held on to it really tightly.

"Don't you like it?" Wanda asked, after a few minutes of everyone waiting for Sir Horace to say something.

"**I have always liked this sword,**" he said in a peculiar voice.

"What does he mean—'always'?" Wanda whispered to me. "He just got it."

Sir Horace made a kind of gulping noise and carried on, "**My dear father gave this sword to me on my twenty-first** birthday. And you have returned it to me on my five-hundredth birthday. Thank you. . . ."

I was disappointed. It's not a proper birthday present if you give someone something that already belongs to them.

But Sir Horace didn't seem to mind. **"This . . . is the best present I could possibly have,"** he said. He sat down on a chair in the corner and carefully propped up the sword beside him. I am sure I heard him sniff, although Wanda says he can't have, because ghosts don't cry— but I don't see how she is such an expert.

On the way upstairs to our Sunday bedroom, we saw something really odd. A long trail of our green string came out from under the secret passage door and went all the way downstairs and into the broom closet.

"That's our string," yawned Wanda.

"I wonder what it's doing there?"

But I was too sleepy to answer.

The next morning we followed the string down to the broom closet. We wanted to say a proper happy birthday to Sir Horace.

"Good morning, Sir Horace," we said. "Many happy returns of the day."

Sir Horace sounded puzzled. **"But it is you who have had the happy returns,"** he said.

He was still sitting in the corner with the sword propped up beside him, but now there was a big pile of rust by his feet. We hardly recognized the sword from the night before—it was gleaming. The handle was shiny, and the patterns that we had seen under the rust looked beautiful and shone with inlaid gold. There was a huge ruby set into the top (which Sir Horace called the pommel) and two smaller ones set into the sides. The blade was a bit jagged, though—you could tell that Sir Horace had done a lot of fighting with it—but he had polished it so well that it was now smooth, glittering steel.

"'Morning Minty, Wanda," said Uncle Drac, yawning. "Sleep well?"

"Yes, thank you, Uncle Drac," we said.

"Good," said Uncle Drac, "because I didn't. That ridiculous sword. I told Sir H to go and scrape the rust off somewhere else, but he sat here all night, scrape, scrape, scrape. Set my teeth on edge something rotten."

"Sorry, Uncle Drac," I said.

"Don't worry about it, Minty." Uncle Drac smiled. "It's worth it just to have you both home safe and sound. Pass me my knitting, will you?"

I gave Uncle Drac his long green scarf. It was just as I had thought. Uncle Drac was knitting our green string.

"Do you know why your yarn feels really scratchy, Uncle Drac?" I asked him.

"I blame Big Bat," Uncle Drac grumbled. "I was knitting so fast yesterday—after you and Wanda disappeared—that I ran out of wool. I told the dumb bat to find me some more green wool and he came back with this old stuff. Don't know where he found it."

"We do," we said.

That afternoon, Sir Horace had his birthday party. It was a great party, even though it wasn't a surprise. Wanda had gone down the secret passage all on her own to find Edmund and ask him to the party. I was amazed, as I thought she didn't like the secret passage because of all the spiders. But Wanda said that she didn't care what was in there anymore, as long as it wasn't seaweed.

We all squeezed into the broom closet and sang "Happy Birthday to You," then Sir Horace bowed and sang "Happy Birthday" back to us. Barry's frogs did what Barry called their famous frog pyramid, which just looked like a pile of frogs to me. Then Barry tried to make Uncle Drac disappear—but all that happened was Uncle Drac got covered in blue disappearing dust and started to sneeze. Brenda did a weird tap dance while spinning some plates on sticks, but all the plates fell off when Uncle Drac gave a really big sneeze and everyone went "Eurgh!" But the best part was when Aunt Tabby and Brenda brought in the five-hundredth birthday cake. It was huge—it had to be to fit all the candles. The candles were so hot that the icing melted, but the cake tasted great all the same. After that Sir Horace fell asleep, so we all tiptoed out and left Uncle Drac to listen to his snores.

Sir Horace was happy after his birthday. He stopped hiding away and even started humming as he walked through the house, which was not such a good thing, as we got a little tired of Sir Horace humming "Happy Birthday to You" all the time—but at least we could hear him coming now.

Uncle Drac carried on knitting while his legs got better. Wanda and I got Uncle Drac

a whole pile of new green yarn, and now we both have really weird, lumpy green scarves.

It took Barry a whole week to get brave enough to tell Uncle Drac about Old Morris and the bat poo, and he was really surprised when Uncle Drac said he didn't care—he was going into the scarf-knitting business. Wanda snorted and said, "Lumpy scarf-knitting business, you mean."

Brenda let us keep the green string, as it

was all ragged from where Big Bat had chewed it off the door. So we wound it up and hung it on the inside of the secret passage door—ready for the next time.

ANGIE SAGE, the celebrated author of the Septimus Heap series, shares her house with three ghosts who are quite shy. Two of the ghosts walk up and down the hall every now and then, while the other one sits and looks at the view out of the window. All three are just about the nicest ghosts you would ever wish to meet. She lives in England. You can visit her online at www.septimusheap.com.

JIMMY PICKERING studied film and character animation and has worked for Hallmark, Disney, and Universal Studios. He is the illustrator of several picture books. You can visit him online at www.jimmypickering.com.

For exclusive information on your favorite authors and artists, visit www.authortracker.com.